The Purple Ribbon

The Purple Ribbon

Sharelle Byars Moranville

ILLUSTRATED BY Anna Alter

HENRY HOLT AND COMPANY ❧ NEW YORK

To my aunt Doris and Christy Ottaviano
—S. B. M.

For my nana Madeline
—A. A.

Henry Holt and Company, LLC
Publishers since 1866
115 West 18th Street
New York, New York 10011
www.henryholt.com

Library of Congress Cataloging-in-Publication Data
Moranville, Sharelle Byars.
The purple ribbon / Sharelle Byars Moranville; illustrated by Anna Alter.
p.   cm.
Summary: An heirloom purple ribbon winds its way through the tale of Spring,
a field mouse, who grows up in her grandmother's nest in a thorn tree
on top of a hill, leaves to bear her own family, and yearns to return home.
[1. Mice—Fiction. 2. Ribbons—Fiction. 3. Family life—Fiction.
4. Heirlooms—Fiction.] I. Alter, Anna, ill. II. Title.
PZ7.M78825 Pu 2003   [Fic]—dc21   2002004039
ISBN 0-8050-6659-4 / First Edition—2003 / Designed by Donna Mark
Printed in Hong Kong
1 3 5 7 9 10 8 6 4 2

The artist used watercolor, colored pencil, and pen and ink on BFK Rives
printmaking paper to create the illustrations for this book.

Contents

Thorn tree

Flower bed

The woods

Blackberry
hedge

Shed

Pond

The Purple Ribbon

CHAPTER ONE

The Beetle

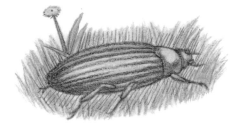

Spring twisted stems of chamomile into a crown and watched the shiny black beetle. When the beetle lumbered left into the grass, Spring followed.

First the beetle led her along an old board that the termites had turned into a trail of streams and pools and caves. Then he meandered around a pair of boots clotted with mud. The beetle turned right at the watering can and ambled into the end of the garden hose.

Spring stayed close behind, even though her crown got knocked off and the walls of the tunnel pressed against her back.

It was dark and tight in the garden hose, and Spring decided she shouldn't have followed the beetle so closely. She could hear him moving on ahead of her, but she herself was stuck. She squirmed and twisted, her whiskers getting all scrunched.

Spring could feel the sunshine warming her tail, which stuck out the end of the garden hose. She tried to yell for her gran. "GranDora!" she called. "Help!"

But her body corked the end of the hose so tightly that not even a whisper escaped. And who knew where her words would come out at the other end? Probably far, far away. Probably in a place so far away that GranDora would never go there, never hear Spring's cries.

Would Spring be stuck in the garden hose all day? All night? Forever?

"Help!" she yelled again.

Maybe GranDora would come along and see Spring's tail sticking out. Sometimes GranDora ran by this end of the garden hose on her way home from gathering seeds.

But would GranDora notice a tail that was lying there all pink and warm in the sunshine? Or would she just trot right over it, anxious to get to their home under the thorn tree?

Spring felt a coolness brush her tail. She held very still.

Maybe a drifting cloud made a shadow that wandered over her tail. Maybe Something Else made the

shadow—Something Else with a beak and talons sharp as knives, who carried mice away and ate them.

GranDora had told Spring about hawks, how they screamed when they lunged. Spring listened, though she was wedged so tightly in the hose that she might as well have had beeswax in her ears.

But something definitely had hold of her tail. Spring squeezed her eyes shut, waiting.

Something pulled very hard—so hard that Spring thought her tail would come off. What if something carried away her tail, like a plump worm, to a nest high up on the cliffs of the riverbank?

How would GranDora, or anybody else, ever find Spring stuck in the garden hose without her tail?

Then, in a burst of sunshine and a rush of wind, Spring popped out of the garden hose!

GranDora's whiskers drooped with tiredness. Her bundle of chamomile scattered in the breeze, and her gray brow furrowed as she dragged Spring clear of the hose.

"Oh, Gran, I thought something had my tail," Spring said, bouncing up and smoothing her fur.

"I thought something had you!" Gran said. "How did you get in there?"

"I followed a shiny black beetle," Spring replied, picking up her crushed chamomile crown and shaping it to fit her gran's head.

The crown made her gran look less tired and cranky. Spring tucked in a scilla blossom for good measure. Already Gran was smiling again.

"Now you're a queen wearing her crown," Spring said. "And you get to do anything you want to do. Would you like to follow a beetle?"

"No," Gran said, rubbing dirt off Spring's ear. "I'd like to go home. Straight home." And she trotted off, leading the way through the grass.

Spring had no choice but to follow the queen, even though she saw the shiny black beetle again and wondered where he was going.

CHAPTER TWO

The Purple Ribbon

Spring wriggled under her gran's tidy bed of oak leaves and squirrel fur. She was looking for the other end of the purple ribbon.

"Spring? What are you doing?" her gran asked.

Spring peeked out. GranDora was twisting her tail into a pin curl, getting ready for bed.

"Why is my bed rolling like grass in the wind?" GranDora asked.

Spring shimmied out, holding the purple ribbon high. One end of the ribbon still clung to something, so Spring gave it a yank.

"Gran! Did you know you had a purple ribbon under your bed?"

GranDora clapped her paws over her eyes as the

bed raveled out and squirrel fur billowed across the floor of their home between the roots of the old thorn tree.

"Oh, my fine bed that I was just going to climb into." Gran's voice said she'd had a long day and her paws hurt. Gran's look said, Oh my, Spring . . . not more mischief. . . .

Spring brushed dust off her velvety brown fur. "But see what I found, Gran."

GranDora shut her eyes, looking as if she were counting to four. "Be careful, Spring. That ribbon is an heirloom."

Spring waltzed around the room, twirling the ribbon. "But where did you get it, Gran? What's it doing on the bottom of our bed? May I keep it now that I found it? I'll be careful. Don't worry."

"Don't worry?" GranDora's brows rose almost to her ears.

Spring buried her face in the ribbon. She knew what Gran was thinking. She was thinking about the careless things Spring had done when she was little. But Spring was older now, and much more responsible.

"Don't worry," Spring said again. Gran would just have to trust her to be more careful.

She twisted the purple ribbon around GranDora's gray head and kissed her gran's soft ear. "Please?" Spring asked.

"No, Spring. You can't have it," GranDora said.

Spring's brow wrinkled.

"Come," GranDora said. "It's bedtime."

Why did bedtime seem to show up at the most interesting part of the day?

"You may hold the purple ribbon while you fall asleep," GranDora told her.

With a sigh, Spring climbed onto the broken-down bed. GranDora curled beside her and draped the purple streamer across their shoulders.

She petted Spring's ears. "My mother gave me the purple ribbon. And her mother gave it to her," GranDora

said as Spring watched the night shapes move across the walls. "And who knows how many generations back our purple ribbon goes?"

She told Spring about the relatives who had moved away to the strawberry patch or gone to live in the mulch pile under the pines. She told her about the relatives who had been eaten by hawks or snakes or owls or cats, and recited their names.

"And that's why we treasure our heirlooms," Gran-Dora said, rubbing her chin against the top of Spring's head as the night wind sang in the dried grass. "Because they tie us to our families."

"We could tie me to our family," Spring said. "With the purple ribbon."

GranDora kissed the top of Spring's head but didn't answer. Spring stroked the purple ribbon, hoping Gran was about to change her mind. Couldn't she see that Spring became more grown up every day?

They lay quietly, listening to the soft rumble of moles passing by. Spring breathed in the sweet smell of clover drying in the corner.

Just when she decided her gran had fallen asleep, GranDora's nose twitched, as if in a dream, and she hugged Spring. "You may have the purple ribbon," she said.

A star winked at Spring through a crack in the wall. Spring winked back.

"But when you're grown up," GranDora added. "I will give it to you when you're all grown up."

Spring yawned. Oh, well. She could wait.

She wrapped herself in the purple ribbon against the night chill, happy that someday it would be hers.

CHAPTER THREE

The Babies

Spring did grow up. She thought it took forever, but GranDora said it took no more time than a falling star's swish through the night sky. And GranDora kept her promise and gave Spring the purple ribbon.

One mild winter day, when the snow had melted and left the earth soft and rich with seeds, Spring went out to forage. She wore a necklace of pink clover and the purple ribbon tied around her ample middle.

The sun brushed her shoulders as she dashed around the woods, searching for seeds. She ran from the brambles to the roots of the mulberry tree, then into the

shadow of the juniper. Following the blackberry hedge that wandered down the hill, Spring drifted farther and farther from the thorn tree.

She found so many seeds that she didn't even look up when a squirrel dashed across her path and chattered something. She didn't notice the gray blanket of cloud covering the sun until a wet, fluffy snowflake plopped on her head.

Then she looked up. When had the sky grown so dark?

She scrambled to the top of a leaf mound for a better view. Through a stinging wind of snow, she could barely see the thorn tree, far away, on top of the hill.

GranDora would be worried. Spring was expecting her babies any day, and GranDora didn't like for her to leave the hilltop.

A lash of wind stung Spring's face and knocked her off the leaf mound. Her necklace ripped loose and blew into the blackberry vines.

Spring wanted to get home and let GranDora dry her fur and pet her ears and bring her warm tea. She tried to run back up the hill, but before she got to the next thicket, the hilltop disappeared into a cloud of swirling snow, and a cut of wind bowled her over.

How would Spring ever get home in time to have her babies? Tumbling along in the wind, she rolled and

skidded down the hill. She saw a shed, with snow already drifting against the side, and she shot through a crack in the boards.

Inside, the wind did not blow so loudly. Clots of snow dropped off Spring as she looked around.

She darted under a dusty old car and sniffed the air. Where would be a warm, safe place to make her nest?

Spring ran up the curve of the car's flat tire. Ducking under a cobweb, she leapt onto a fender ledge. She squeaked through a crack and trotted along a red cable under the hood. When the cable ended, she dropped to the floor of the car, so thin and rusty in places that she could see through it. But under the seat would be a marvelous place to build her nest—warm and safe.

Spring sat for a minute, catching her breath. Then

she leapt back onto the cable and squirmed through the crack. She dropped off the fender ledge onto the tire and tumbled down its curve to the floor. She must hurry.

Spring gathered up strands of black dog hair from the floor of the shed. Carrying the first load, she dashed up the tire, onto the ledge, through the crack, and down the red cable. With a heave, she pitched the dog hair into a pile. Then, without stopping to rest, Spring trotted back.

Over and over, she made the trip, growing very tired and hungry. But she didn't stop until she had a thick mattress of black hair. In a flurry of weaving, she tucked and tied strands of hair so the nest wouldn't fly apart.

When that was done, Spring charged along the cable again. In the corner of the shed, behind a pile of cardboard boxes, she found a cache of plastic foam peanuts and nibbled them with her teeth until her cheeks bulged. With her load, Spring wobbled back to the nest and poked the tiny white cushions into the webs of woven hair.

After many, many trips, Spring had built a nest with a soft black bottom and a bouncy white top. She stood back, proud of her work, wishing GranDora could see it.

Spring made one last trip for a chunk of dog food that she had noticed on the shed floor. Lugging the dog food back to her nest, she rested on the fender ledge for a moment. Then she squirmed through the crack and ran, puffing, along the cable. At last, she settled into her nest.

During the night, warm under the seat of the car, Spring wove the purple ribbon into her nest for safe-keeping. She gnawed on the dog food. She thought about GranDora and her home under the thorn tree. And she had her babies.

In the morning, four baby mice snuggled in the nest under the front seat of the old car.

Spring named the sturdy boys Oak and Pebble. The girl she called Parsley Snowflake. And the tiniest boy, the one who still lay curled in a little pink mound with his eyes shut, she called Jellybean.

The new mother lay back in the nest, petting her babies, proud that they were safe.

Wrapping one end of the purple ribbon around herself and her babies, Spring daydreamed. Someday she'd take her little ones home to live in the shade of the thorn tree. But for now, they would be a family of car mice.

CHAPTER FOUR

The Bad, Bad, Bad, Bad, Bad Mice

Spring and her four babies settled into their new home. Parsley Snowflake, Oak, and Pebble grew strong on their mother's milk, but tiny Jellybean slept most of the day.

"What's wrong with him, Mama?" Parsley Snowflake asked one morning. "Why doesn't he play?"

"Sometimes babies are just born too tiny," Spring answered, rocking Jellybean. "If we take extra-good care of him, maybe someday he'll catch up with the rest of you."

"I hope so," Parsley Snowflake said, kissing her baby brother between the ears. Then she ran to the edge of the nest with Oak and Pebble to look at the great world beyond.

Overhead, the young ones saw the sprung bottom of the car seat, which their mama had said was not nearly as nice as the sky.

"What's sky, Mama?" Oak asked.

"Tonight I will show you," Spring answered. "I'll take you with me to gather seeds."

"What's in the shadows, Mama?" Pebble wondered aloud, looking deep into the back of the car.

"Nothing much," Spring told him.

"But what, exactly?" Oak asked. "I hear things." And he and Pebble twisted their tails together.

"Sometimes you can hear the wind," Spring said. "It whistles through the cracks. But we're perfectly safe inside this old car."

"Yes, we are," Parsley Snowflake chimed in. "I'm not afraid."

"What's down that hole?" Pebble asked, hanging over the edge of the nest and peering through a hole in the floorboard.

"Oh, just dust and stuff," Parsley Snowflake said, stroking Jellybean's whiskers. "And wind." She looked at her mama to see if that was right.

"I think you better come and see, Mama," Oak said. "I don't think it's dust. Or wind."

All the mice, except Jellybean, hung their heads over the side of the nest to look.

Something large, its eyes fixed on the mice, gazed up through the hole.

Spring yanked her little ones back so quickly they nearly flew out of the other side of the nest.

"What is it, Mama?" Parsley Snowflake cried.

A paw, as thick as Spring herself, explored the hole.

"Shhhhh," Spring whispered as the claws opened over them.

She inched Jellybean back.

The claws grabbed, then disappeared. But the mice could hear a rumbling through the hole.

"That's not the wind, is it, Mama?" Oak whispered.

"Or dust," Pebble said.

"That's a cat," Spring told them. "One of our enemies."

"What's an enemy?" Oak asked.

"Something that wants to eat us," Parsley Snowflake said. "Right, Mama?"

Spring nodded.

Oak and Pebble twined their tails together.

"Has it gone away?" Pebble dared to ask when only a deep silence came up through the hole.

"No," Spring said. "Cats are patient."

After a while, when the mice had been so still they might have been little gray rocks, Spring whispered, "We must drive it away somehow."

"But how, Mama?" Oak asked. "It's a lot bigger than we are."

"Then we must be smarter," Spring said.

"Maybe we could drop something on it," Pebble offered. "If we had something to drop."

"I guess we could try to scare it," Parsley Snowflake said. "We could make noises."

"We need a weapon," Oak decided.

"There's a thorn in the back of the car," Spring said. "Maybe we could poke it with the thorn."

"Yes," Parsley Snowflake agreed. "Poke its paw."

Just then the paw, like a giant, hairy periscope looking

for the tiny mouse family, came up through the hole again.

It was all the little ones could do not to scream. But Spring held up her hand, warning them to be quiet.

After the paw disappeared and they could hear the disgusted rumble of the beast, waiting, Spring whispered, "Stay away from the hole. And watch Jellybean." Quickly, she leapt over the side of the nest and disappeared into the shadows.

Soon she came back, lugging and dragging and scooting the thorn.

"If we all carry it," she said, "we'll be able to ram the paw."

So the four mice gripped the thorn and waited.

They were starting to think the cat had gone away when the paw, stealthy and dangerous, snaked up through the hole again.

"Now," whispered Spring. "CHARGE!"

And the mice ran forward, ramming the cat's paw with the shiny, hooked point of the thorn.

The claws flared and, with a great yowl, the cat raced away.

"Well, my babies," Spring said, dusting off her fur. "You were very brave and very smart. I don't think we need to worry about that cat sticking his old paw up through our hole anymore."

"I'll bet that cat thinks mice are dangerous," Pebble said.

"And we are," Parsley Snowflake agreed. "We're the meanest mice in the world when something tries to eat us."

"Yes, we are," Oak said. And he and Pebble danced around Jellybean, singing, "We are bad, bad, bad, bad, bad."

CHAPTER FIVE

Light Bloom

*T*hat night, Spring got ready to take some of the young ones out to gather seeds. She tucked Jellybean into a cozy corner of the nest and covered him with the purple ribbon.

"We can't leave our littlest one by himself," she said, stroking Jellybean's ears. "He might worry." She looked at Parsley Snowflake. "I know I can trust you to stay with him."

Parsley Snowflake swallowed. She wanted to see the sky and the stars that their mama had told them about.

"I'll take you soon," Spring promised. "To a special meadow."

"Then I'll stay with Jellybean," Parsley Snowflake said. "I'll make up stories about the stars for him."

Oak and Pebble ran around in circles, waiting for Spring.

"We're going to see the sky—"

"—And the moon—"

"—And more seeds than we can even imagine. And the leaves and puddles—"

"Good-bye, my sweets," Spring said to Parsley Snowflake and Jellybean. "Back soon."

And she led the way to the red cable.

"We'll make a chain with our tails until we get through the passageway," she told Oak and Pebble. "Be still, now. And stop bouncing around."

In a wiggly line, the three mice trotted along the cable until they came to the crack in the wall. Spring motioned the little ones to follow her, and they shimmied through it.

On the other side, Pebble whispered, "Where are we?"

"Shhhhh!" Spring said. "We're almost out."

She pushed aside a dusty cobweb, then vanished.

"Where's Mama?" Oak said, forgetting to whisper. "Mama! —ama! —ama!" His voice echoed under the hood of the car.

"Shhhh!" Spring said, her head appearing from below the fender ledge. "Down here."

And she helped both of the little mice onto the top of the tire.

"Now we'll run and then jump," she said. "Follow me."

So the three mice raced down the tire, then leapt through the air, landing on the floor.

Spring led the way through a crack in a board.

"Oh, Mama," Oak said, looking up at the starry canopy. "That must be the sky."

"And these are leaves," Pebble said, first rolling on one, then jumping up and down and making it crackle. "Right, Mama?"

"And these are seeds," Oak said. "Look. I found one. And there's another one." And he ran off, following a trail of seeds up a leaf mound.

Pebble ran along behind him.

"Look at the stars," Pebble said. "Look at the extra-bright one shining just over the treetop. I'm going to name it Light Bloom."

"But it's not yours," Pebble said. "I saw it first. So you don't get to name it."

"Yes, I do," Oak said. "Its name is Light Bloom."

"Mama—" Pebble began.

"My babies," Spring said, "don't squabble over the stars. Come with me, and I'll show you something even more wonderful."

And they followed her up to the top of the leaf mound.

"Look," Spring said. And she pointed to the hill. The big thorn tree, its branches swaying in the wind, made the stars seem to flicker and dance.

"My GranDora lives in a fine home between the roots of that great tree," Spring said. "Someday we'll return."

A barn owl cried in the field and Spring rushed the little ones back into the shed.

On the return trip through the passage, Oak and Pebble raced ahead, leading their mama. And when they got back to the nest, they told Parsley Snowflake and Jellybean about everything they had seen and done.

CHAPTER SIX

Down the Hole

One sunny March day, when the snow had all turned to slush and the winter wind had worn itself out, the mice felt a burst of air as the car door opened.

A voice boomed, "Well, Harry, let's see if the old heap will still start."

A giant leather boot mashed down, inches from the mice. As the front seat sank over their heads, Spring, Parsley Snowflake, Oak, and Pebble leapt from the nest.

"This is *our* car," Oak cried, tumbling over his own feet, then standing up.

"Here goes nothing," the man said.

A grinding and groaning came from under the hood. Then, with an explosion of noise, the car bucked and began to shake.

The mice looked at one another. The vibration made their teeth rattle and their noses itch and the world go blurry.

"You-u-u-u l-l-l-l-ook fun-n-n-ny," Pebble said to Oak.

"You-u-u-u tal-l-l-l-k fun-n-n-ny," Oak said to Pebble.

"Stop acting sil-l-y," Parsley Snowflake told them.

"Jellybean!" Spring cried, staring at the nest as it shimmied toward the hole in the floor.

They could see Jellybean's tail sticking up in fear, but he wasn't strong enough to jump out of the nest.

"What will we do?" Parsley Snowflake said, watching the nest inch nearer and nearer the hole.

The vibration was sending them *all* nearer and nearer the hole.

"Run," Pebble said.

"Run away from the hole," Oak said.

Parsley Snowflake leapt into the nest and tugged the purple ribbon tightly around Jellybean's middle.

"Don't be afraid," she told him, then she said the same thing to herself as the jagged, rusty edge of the hole gaped closer. "I've got you," she whispered, squeezing him.

She threw out the other end of the ribbon. "Pull!" she cried.

Spring, Oak, and Pebble tugged, throwing all their weight against the ribbon.

Jellybean stared at Parsley Snowflake with trusting eyes as stinky air from the hole eddied around them.

"Here we go," Parsley Snowflake said, hoisting him over the edge of the nest as her mother and brothers heaved against the rope of ribbon. "U-u-p and over."

And they were out of the nest.

Scrambling and dragging Jellybean in a loop of ribbon, they made their way to safety beneath the rear seat.

They looked back just in time to see the nest tilt over the hole. Everybody gave Jellybean about a thousand kisses as Spring untied him.

Oak and Pebble danced around.

"We did it! We did it!" they cried.

The car didn't shake nearly as much in the rear, and there was no hole for a cat's paws to snake through. All five mice were still together.

And then the car stopped with one last buck and blast.

"Not too bad," the voice boomed. "A little backfiring. But at least she still starts."

CHAPTER SEVEN

Bouncers and Flippers

One morning a few weeks later, when the smell of daffodils drifted into the car, Parsley Snowflake, Oak, and Pebble stacked acorn caps into mountains under the backseat while their mama sat in the nest, nursing Jellybean.

After the near disaster, they'd spent a long time taking apart their old nest and moving the pieces into a warm corner far under the backseat. Then their mama had nipped and tucked and woven until the nest was as good as new.

"Look," Oak said to Parsley Snowflake. "My mountain is bigger than yours."

"Not anymore," she replied as it tumbled down.

"Hey!" he yelled. "You knocked my mountain-n-n-n do-o-o-own."

"D-i-i-i-d not," she said.

"We're moving," cried Pebble.

They lurched into each other as the car jerked and shot backward.

"You better get in the nest," Spring called to them.

The car jerked again and went forward, and the three little mice rolled into their acorn cups.

"Hurry," Spring said.

Parsley Snowflake, Oak, and Pebble leapt in.

Then the car hit a pothole, and the mice bounced so high that they were in a different order when they came down.

"Hey!" Pebble shook his head and brushed fluff off his ears. "That was fun."

"Maybe the car will do it again," Oak said.

And it did.

This time Oak turned a somersault in the air, and Pebble pretended to fly, knocking the wind out of himself when he landed on his stomach.

The car hit a whole lot of bumps, and the mice bounced like trampoline artists.

"Look," Spring said as she touched her toes in the air.

The young ones all clapped.

"What a bouncer you are, Mama," Parsley Snowflake said.

Then Spring did a backward flip, and everybody clapped again.

Jellybean's eyes sparkled as he watched his family shoot into the air like popping corn.

"You are a dandy, dandy mouse," Parsley Snowflake said, unwrapping Jellybean from the belt of purple ribbon. She held on to him as they bounced from one side of the nest to the other.

"Be careful with him," Spring said, just as the car stopped bouncing and began to go faster. "Maybe we should all wrap up in the purple ribbon for a while. Who knows what the car is going to do next!"

So she lined up her little ones around the edge of the nest and cinched them all under the broad band of the purple ribbon.

The car went fast for a while, and then it went slow, and then it stopped and did boring car things. The mice played games and snacked on some cornmeal they'd carried back to the nest last night. As they settled in for a nap beneath the purple ribbon, Spring told them about the heirloom.

"My gran gave me this," she said, smoothing the ribbon over Jellybean. "And her mama gave it to her. *And her mama gave it to her.* And who knows how many generations back the purple ribbon goes!"

Oak was tying Pebble's tail into a knot. Pebble had fallen asleep. Parsley Snowflake was twisting one end of the purple ribbon around her head, trying to make a bonnet.

None of the little ones answered Spring's question.

She smiled. "I've raised a family of car mice," she said. "What would GranDora say if she could see you?"

And then the car slowed down and, with much bumping and rocking, pulled back into the shed.

That night, Spring left Jellybean, who had grown stronger, with Oak and Pebble. As she had promised, she took Parsley Snowflake on her first trip into the great world beyond the nest.

"Oh, Mama," Parsley Snowflake said, gazing at the sky and stars. "It's wonderful."

Spring led her to a small meadow where toadstools arched over them like white umbrellas shading the moonlight.

"You never told us about these," Parsley Snowflake said, leaping onto a baby toadstool.

"I saved a surprise just for you," Spring said, leading the way as they leapt from toadstool to toadstool, getting ever higher.

"I'll bet I can almost touch the stars," Parsley Snowflake said, looking up.

"Almost," Spring agreed.

As the barn owl cried from across the meadow, Spring told Parsley Snowflake about the danger of snakes and hawks and owls and cats, and recited a long list of relatives who had been eaten by one or another.

"Someday we'll go home," Spring said. She gazed at the thorn tree, where the shadow of the great thorny branches seemed to make cracks on the ground. "A car isn't really the best place to raise a family. It's very unpredictable."

CHAPTER EIGHT

The Creature That Flew Backward

As the days grew warmer and the nights grew shorter, Spring let Parsley Snowflake, Oak, and Pebble go out alone to play in the shade of the lilac bush.

One day, Parsley Snowflake saw a strange winged creature drop out of the sky and skim a puddle left by the booming thunderstorm the night before.

"Look out!" she yelled.

Oak and Pebble shot into the grass. Parsley Snowflake dove under the overhang of a fat lilac blossom.

"Is it a hawk?" Pebble's voice sounded far away.

"Is it an owl?" Oak called from a thick clump of blue lime grass.

Parsley Snowflake wasn't sure, but she didn't think so.

Its four wings sparkled as if the purple glitter of puddles in the twilight had been brushed on them.

Could something as bad as a hawk be so beautiful?

"I think it's something else," Parsley Snowflake called to her brothers.

"Something else?" Oak said.

"Like what, exactly?" Pebble asked.

"I don't know," Parsley Snowflake said, unable to take her gaze off the fabulous creature. It darted through the sunshine so fast, her eyes could hardly follow it.

It hovered over the puddle, its wings brushing the air with purple light.

"It can fly standing still," Parsley Snowflake reported to the grass. "Can hawks do that?"

"I don't think so," Oak said. "What else can it do?"

"Well . . ." Parsley Snowflake slid out from under the blossom to get a better look.

The creature must have seen her with its enormous bulbous eyes. It shot backward over the water.

"And guess what," Parsley Snowflake yelled. "It can fly backward."

"Fly backward?" Oak's voice came from the clump of grass. "Are you sure?"

"Come and see," Parsley Snowflake said. "I don't think it eats mice."

The grass parted and Pebble's nose appeared.

Just then, the wiry winged creature shot straight up and hovered, silhouetted against the sun.

"Where'd it go?" Pebble asked, stepping out of the grass. "I don't see anything."

"Are you making this up?" Oak grumbled, also slipping out of the shelter of the tall grass.

"Look." Parsley Snowflake pointed into the sun. "Up there."

Oak's and Pebble's heads went back. All at once the creature dropped straight down and a fat, black fly that had been droning low and slow over the puddle disappeared.

"Wow," Oak marveled.

Then the creature hovered right in front of them, seeming to watch the three mice as they scurried under the leaf. It dipped its wings, shot straight up and down two or three times, and zipped backward, out of sight.

"Wow," Oak said again.

"Bye, Thing," Parsley Snowflake called out.

———

"So what was it, Mama?" Oak asked that night, after they'd gathered seeds and brought them back to the nest. They were settling down under the purple ribbon and had told Spring about the fantastic creature that flew backward. "Was it a hawk?"

"Were its four wings as narrow as blades of grass?" Spring asked.

The three mice nodded.

"Were they clear and shiny and blue, like water in the twilight?" Spring asked.

"Just exactly like that," Parsley Snowflake said.

"Were its eyes as big as peas?"

"Yes," said Parsley Snowflake. "Maybe bigger."

"Well, then," Spring said, tucking the little ones in, "that's easy. It was a dragonfly."

"A dragonfly?" questioned Oak.

Spring pulled the ribbon up to her chin and gazed around the nest at her little ones. "Let me tell you what else dragonflies are called. They're called pond hawks."

The children looked at their mama, and they looked at each other, remembering what had happened to the fat, black fly.

"And that," Spring said, "is why I want you to be careful."

CHAPTER NINE

The Trip

Summertime blossomed into long, hot, hazy days. One morning, sleepily, Parsley Snowflake watched her mama tuck the purple ribbon under Jellybean's chin, then slip out of the nest into the early morning quiet.

Not long after Spring left, Parsley Snowflake heard the shed door roll open. Trying not to wake her brothers, Parsley Snowflake scrambled from the nest, up the seat, and onto the car's window ledge. Outside, a narrow line of pink streaked the pearl gray sky, and she saw her mama cutting through the grass to the flower bed.

Parsley Snowflake watched her mama pile cleome seeds under a leaf, pick up a fat maple spinner, and head back toward the nest.

Just then, the car door opened and slammed shut.

Parsley Snowflake willed her mama to hurry back.

The car growled and bucked and began to roll back-ward, then it surged forward, nearly tumbling Parsley Snowflake off the ledge.

She clung to a tuft of stuffing and watched out the window as Spring raced, trying to catch the car. But Spring's legs were too short.

"Good-bye, Mama," Parsley Snowflake whispered.

They had never gone on a car trip without their mama before, and Parsley Snowflake trembled.

Normally she would have loved sitting on the window ledge, watching the clouds and birds and trees, but without her mama she felt lonely. So she went down and woke her brothers and told them she would be the mama for a while.

"Oh yeah?" Oak muttered. "Well, what's Jellybean going to eat?"

Already that was worrying Parsley Snowflake. She hoped the car wouldn't be gone long. Sometimes its trips were very short.

When Jellybean woke up, Parsley Snowflake bounced him and told him he was a dandy mouse. Pebble did tumbling tricks off the edge of the nest, landing with a leap and a shout in front of Jellybean each time.

Jellybean wiggled with delight. But he looked hungry.

After a while, the car slowed down, stopped, and became quiet.

"Stay here," Parsley Snowflake said. And she ran up to look out the rear window.

Parsley Snowflake hoped she would see the grass and the familiar puddles of home. She hoped she would see her mama waiting for them in the shed. But instead, she saw lots of colors and shapes she didn't understand.

She ran back down to the nest.

"Are we home?" Pebble asked.

"No," said Parsley Snowflake.

"Where are we?" Oak asked.

"Someplace else," Parsley Snowflake answered.

"I'm hungry," Pebble said after a while, and left the nest to eat from a pile of seeds the mice had carried to the car the night before.

"What about Jellybean?" Oak said after he, too, had eaten some of the seeds.

"Mama will nurse him when we get home," Parsley Snowflake assured him, trying not to think about how hungry Jellybean looked or when they might get home.

As the time crawled by, Parsley Snowflake rocked Jellybean and tickled him with her whiskers. Finally he fell asleep.

Then the other three mice lay in the nest, not feeling like rolling acorn caps or chasing each other or doing any of the things they usually did while Jellybean had his afternoon nap.

"I wonder where we are," Pebble whispered, tying and retying his tail into a knot.

"I wonder when we'll go back," Oak whispered. "If we ever will."

"The shed is the car's nest," Parsley Snowflake said, speaking more bravely than she felt. "So it will go back."

"Does the car have a mama?" Pebble asked after a few minutes.

"Doesn't everything have a mama?" Parsley Snowflake said, swallowing the lump in her throat.

"Then where does the car's mama live?" Pebble asked.

"I don't know," Parsley Snowflake said. "Maybe it has its own nest."

Oak laid his chin on his paws. "Let's not talk about mamas anymore," he sighed.

While the afternoon passed, Parsley Snowflake ran up to look out the rear window several times. The shadows grew longer and Jellybean grew hungrier.

Finally the car swayed and a drift of dust settled over the mice as the door banged closed.

"Here we go!" Parsley Snowflake cheered.

"Home," Pebble said, raising his head.

Oak turned a somersault and tweaked Jellybean's ear. "We're going home!"

And before long, they felt the familiar bumps and

ruts of home, and with a sway the car came to a stand-still in the shed.

"Yaaaaay!" Oak yelled.

"We're home," Pebble told Jellybean, tugging on his tail.

"And we can tell Mama all about our day," Parsley Snowflake said and smiled.

CHAPTER TEN

The Stranger

Later that night, after Jellybean, hungry and cross, had finally fallen asleep, Parsley Snowflake crept to the edge of the nest.

"You stay here," she whispered to Oak and Pebble. "I'll search for Mama."

"Why can't we come?" Pebble asked.

"What if the car leaves again?" Parsley Snowflake said. "Who would look after Jellybean?"

Pebble twined his tail around Oak's. "Will you come back?"

"Yes," Parsley Snowflake told them. And she ran into the darkness.

Outside, stars spattered the sky, and a bright full moon painted the ground with shadows.

What had happened to their mama while they'd been gone? Had she tried to follow the car and had an accident?

Parsley Snowflake ran down the lane. "Mama?" she called.

Sometimes she heard rustling in the grass, but when she explored, she found only a beetle or a toad.

When her legs shook with tiredness and her fur hung thick with burrs, she headed back. Returning on the other side of the lane, for an instant she thought she saw her mama, but it was only the shape of a rock in the moonlight.

Still, she sat down by the rock.

"Mama?" she whispered. "Where are you? Where have you gone? Jellybean's hungry."

After a while, she looked up at the stars.

Then she went to search the flower bed. She checked between all the rows of zinnias and marigolds and cleome and nasturtiums and baby's breath and snap-dragons and cosmos and larkspur and asters.

"Mama?" she called.

She searched around the edge of the mud puddle for signs of her mama's paws. She sat down on the rim of the puddle and watched the reflection of the stars quiver in the water.

She stayed there a long time.

Finally she got up and trudged back toward the shed.

In the deep shadows that marked the edge of the shed, she heard something ahead of her in the darkness.

"Mama! Mama!" she called, racing toward the familiar figure. "Wait!"

The figure stopped and turned around, silhouetted against the moonlight. Then it began to move toward Parsley Snowflake.

Parsley Snowflake, understanding too late, tried to make her legs go in reverse.

It wasn't her mama.

"I've been looking for you," said the stranger.

Parsley Snowflake wheeled on the path.

"Wait, little one. Don't run away. I'm your own GranDora."

Parsley Snowflake paused, hardly daring to believe. "GranDora? Mama's gran?"

The older mouse, dusty and worn out, limped down the path to Parsley Snowflake.

"Where's Mama?" Parsley Snowflake asked.

"Feeding Jellybean," GranDora said.

Parsley Snowflake began to tremble. Mama was in the nest!

GranDora petted her ears. "When your mama got to the thorn tree today, tired to pieces, she said, 'Parsley Snowflake will take care of them. No matter what.'"

Parsley Snowflake couldn't speak. She stared at the

stars for a long time as GranDora kept petting her ears. The stars seemed to dance to the music in her heart.

"Let's go see your mama now," GranDora said. "Before she worries any more."

Parsley Snowflake followed GranDora. As they neared the nest, she could hear Oak and Pebble trying to tell their mama everything.

She leapt into the confusion, nearly knocking Oak over and partly squashing Jellybean. "Oh, Mama, don't ever leave us again."

CHAPTER ELEVEN

The Journey

The next morning, Pebble woke everybody up by doing handstands and kicking his feet in the air, making Jellybean laugh.

"We're moving to GranDora's house," he told Jellybean.

"Under the thorn tree," Pebble added.

"I'm going to take all my acorn balls," Oak said.

"And I'm going to take a big snack," Pebble said.

"I'm going to take Jellybean, wrapped in a cocoon on my back," GranDora declared. And she rolled him up in the purple ribbon.

"Good-bye, nest," Parsley Snowflake said when Jellybean was tied to GranDora's back and Oak stood with his bundle of acorn balls and Pebble carried several stems of hollyhock heads for a snack.

"Good-bye, hole," Oak said as they trekked through the car.

"That old cat nearly got us," Pebble said.

"Good-bye, passageway," Parsley Snowflake said, brushing through the cobweb curtain.

"Good-bye, car," Oak said when they had all scrambled safely down the tire.

Spring tucked the purple ribbon under Jellybean's chin and said, "I'll lead the way."

The sun beat down and insects sang as the family followed Spring along a trail through the grass.

By the time they got across the lane, GranDora walked slowly. So they unwrapped Jellybean and sat a while in the shade, then they tied him to Spring's back and started up the hill.

"Who's going to help me carry my hollyhocks?" Pebble said.

"I will," Parsley Snowflake said, and she took a hollyhock head and began munching.

"Hey!" Pebble said. But then he asked, "Who else wants to help?"

And everybody helped Pebble carry his snacks until there were no more to carry.

Going up the hill was much harder than the first part of the trip. Oak laid down his acorn balls one by one.

"I'm planting trees," he said.

Spring's tail drooped, and the purple ribbon dragged on the ground before they were halfway up the hill.

"We could carry him together," Oak said, pointing to Pebble and Parsley Snowflake. "We could line up side by side."

So for the last part of the long trip up the hill, Jellybean rode on their backs, and they trotted along in step to keep from bouncing him too much.

As they drew close to the base of the thorn tree, deep in the shadows between two roots, they saw the entrance to GranDora's house.

Spring ran ahead, darting into the house, then out again.

"We're home, my little ones, we're home." She raced in a circle around them. "Oh, GranDora, we're home."

CHAPTER TWELVE

Home

In the morning coolness, GranDora, Spring, Parsley Snowflake, and Jellybean watched Oak and Pebble roll around in the great brown seed husks that had fallen from the thorn tree.

GranDora showed Parsley Snowflake how to weave crowns and necklaces from clover, and Spring tried to tidy up the purple ribbon.

"Oh, Gran, look at this poor ribbon," she said, pointing to a large rip. "This happened when we were dragging Jellybean away from the hole. And this—" She pointed to many rips and smudges, using them to tell GranDora the story of her journey.

"So is it still an heirloom?" she asked when she was done. "All ragged and dirty? Or is it ruined?"

GranDora hung a necklace of purple clover around Spring's neck. "It's not ruined," she said. "It's bedraggled, but its meaning is even richer. And it brought you home. You and your babies."

The End